Saving the Curlews

Story by Jill McDougall

Illustrations by Valerie Valdivia

Contents

Chapter 1

A Sign Goes Up

"Let's go!" I said to Archie excitedly. "Come on, hurry up!"

"Give me a minute, Claire," Archie mumbled, as he hunted for his bike helmet.

Although my brother Archie is five years older than me, we are good friends. We both really like funny movies, chocolate chip pancakes and birdwatching.

Birdwatching? *Yes!* That might sound like an unusual hobby for a ten-year-old girl, but let me explain. My home is in a little town called Mud Crab Bay, close to some mudflats. You might think that mudflats don't sound very, er … attractive, and they're not! In fact, the name says it all. Mudflats are flat areas of mud that can only be seen at low tide.

Lots of little crabs hide in the mudflats, and Archie and I like to watch the birds feeding on them. Plus, it's easy to get there on our bikes.

So, why was I telling Archie to hurry up? Great question! The day before, some curlews had arrived on the mudflats! This was the second year we'd seen them, and we knew they were special because we'd looked them up on the internet. They were eastern curlews, and they had flown all the way to Australia from … *dum de dah* … Siberia!

Finally, Archie found his bike helmet, and we rode along the sandy track to the mudflats.

"Someone else is here!" I said, staring at a big green truck in the parking area.

That's when we noticed a man hammering a sign into the ground. It read, "Bay Side Constructions".

"What would anyone want to build out here?" asked Archie, pulling off his helmet.

At that moment, the man's dog bounded towards us. It was small, brown and full of energy.

"That's Snapper," said the man in a friendly voice. "He likes to chase things."

I silently hoped Snapper didn't like to chase curlews, but I smiled politely and patted him.

"I've got good news for you young people," the man said. "In a few weeks, these smelly mudflats will be history!"

"History?" asked Archie, his voice breaking a little.

"That's right!" said the man. "I'm Barry Bragg, and I own Bay Side Constructions. We're going to build a sea wall to stop the tide from covering the mudflats. Then we'll put soil on top of the mud."

I stared at him in amazement. "What's the good news?" I asked.

Barry Bragg flashed me a massive grin (the kind where you see all the teeth). "I'm going to build a holiday park on this site. Instead of mud, there'll be lots of holiday cabins."

At last, I found my voice. "You can't do that!" I blurted out. "What about the birds that feed on these mudflats?"

Barry Bragg gave a hearty laugh, as if I'd made a joke. "Birds!" he said. "Birds can eat anywhere."

But I knew that wasn't true, especially not for the curlews. Yesterday, when they arrived at the mudflats after their long flight, they had looked thin and hungry. Archie and I had watched them gobbling up crabs as if their lives depended on it. Their lives *did* depend on it! They needed the mudflats to survive.

In that moment, I made a silent promise to the curlews. I would save the mudflats!

Chapter 2

Meeting with the Mayor

A few hours later, Archie and I were busy looking up information on the internet about the curlews. Our plan was to print off a fact sheet and take it to the local council to stop the development.

I showed Mum what we had found so far. "The curlews fly 12 000 kilometres to reach Mud Crab Bay," I told her. "They can't glide, so they flap their wings all the way. Isn't that amazing?"

"I bet the council will be impressed," added Archie, scrolling down the web page.

But Mum didn't look too sure. "It's not easy to stop a development once it's been approved," she said, frowning.

Suddenly, Archie let out a low whistle. "Here's something else," he said. "The eastern curlew is endangered! *Critically* endangered!"

It seemed that the curlews were running out of places to feed on their long flight across the globe. Their regular feeding grounds were being replaced with houses and shops and, yes, holiday parks. No wonder the curlews were hungry when they finally reached Mud Crab Bay!

At that moment, I felt a tiny bubble of hope. "Once we explain to Mayor Potter about the curlews being endangered, she's sure to stop the development," I said.

Archie printed off our fact sheet, and Mum drove us to the council building.

"I'll leave you here, and I'll be back shortly to pick you up," said Mum.

As Archie led the way towards the big glass doors, he pointed to a shiny green truck in the car park. The sign on the side of the truck said, "Bay Side Constructions".

"That's Barry Bragg's truck," Archie muttered.

"He got here before us!" I groaned. "He's probably talking to the mayor now. I hope we're not too late!"

At the front desk, we were given some bad news. "Mayor Potter is in a meeting," said a young man, glancing at his computer. "She is very busy this month. Come back in a few weeks."

"But this is an emergency!" I cried. "We need to see Mayor Potter urgently!"

"It's about the new holiday park," added Archie helpfully.

At that moment, a woman poked her head around a door. It was Mayor Potter herself! "Holiday park?" she asked. "You're just in time for the community meeting. Come on in!" she added, looking at Archie and me.

RECEPTION

The meeting room was filled with people who stared at us as we entered. I recognised a few people who owned cafes and shops in Mud Crab Bay. At the front of the room stood Barry Bragg. He was giving a presentation. "We're calling it the Bay Side Holiday Park," Barry Bragg was saying. "It's most exciting!"

"These young people are excited, too," said Mayor Potter, smiling at Archie and me.

I knew I had to say something, even though my stomach was doing cartwheels.

"Actually, we're not excited about the holiday park," I said in one breath.

"Pardon?" said Mayor Potter, looking puzzled.

"There are curlews feeding on the mudflats," explained Archie. "And they're endangered."

Barry Bragg frowned at us. "You're wrong," he said, looking annoyed. "We have an EIS, and there is nothing in it about any endangered … curlings."

"Curlews," Archie corrected him. "And, er … what's an EIS?"

"It stands for Environmental Impact Statement," explained Mayor Potter kindly. "It's a report made by scientists who study the effects a new development might have on the environment." She smiled at us both. "If there were endangered birds on the mudflats, the scientists would have mentioned them in the report."

Archie blew out a long sigh. He looked defeated. "I guess it's hard to argue with an EIS," he said at last. I watched him turn towards the door. "Let's go, Claire. There's nothing more we can do."

Chapter 3

A Light-Bulb Moment

I felt as if I was frozen on the spot. I knew there were curlews on the mudflats. I just *knew* it. We had seen them last year, too. So how had the scientists missed them? Then, suddenly, it came to me.

"When was the EIS report done?" I asked Mayor Potter.

"Last winter," she replied brightly. "The scientists visited the mudflats for three months."

"So there you have it," chimed in Barry Bragg, looking relieved.

"Wait a minute!" I said. I felt as if a light bulb had lit up in my brain. "The curlews aren't on the mudflats in winter. They migrate from Siberia and only spend the warm months here!"

"That's why the scientists didn't see them!" added Archie excitedly.

Barry Bragg's face turned an interesting shade of red, but he kept his voice low. "You children don't understand," he said slowly. "A holiday park will bring tourists to Mud Crab Bay. Tourists are good for business. They spend money in our cafes and shops."

Some of the business people nodded in agreement.

"These kids could have seen seagulls for all we know!" added Barry Bragg with a laugh.

Seagulls! I felt my face flush in frustration. Then I remembered the fact sheet! I held it up so everyone could see it clearly, and pointed to the photo. "These are the birds on the mudflats," I said, as calmly as I could. "They're *eastern* curlews."

Barry Bragg glared at me. “It’s too late,” he said. “The development starts on Monday, and the bulldozers are on their way.”

Mayor Potter was looking thoughtful. “It would be a shame to destroy the habitat of endangered birds,” she said at last. “I’m sure Mr Bragg would agree.” She glanced at Barry Bragg, who was fiddling with his laptop. “Shall we drive out this Sunday and take a look, Barry? We could meet these young people out there.”

Mr Bragg shrugged his shoulders. “Sure,” he said.

Chapter 4

Where Are the Curlews?

On Sunday afternoon, Archie and I rode out to the mudflats to meet Mayor Potter and Barry Bragg. It was the day before the mudflats would be destroyed forever.

Archie and I arrived early. "I hope the curlews are close by," I whispered, as we walked *very* slowly towards the mudflats. The birds were disturbed by the smallest movement, and we didn't want to frighten them.

Archie and I lay on our bellies in the warm sand, and Archie scanned the mudflats with his binoculars. "Seagulls," he muttered. "Plovers … more seagulls."

"Where are the curlews?" I asked anxiously.

"Found them!" whispered Archie, passing the binoculars to me.

Three brown, speckled curlews were stalking across the mudflats. Their long, curved beaks probed the mud for food.

Archie had told me that there was a hidden ecosystem under the mud. It was filled with crabs and shellfish, snails and worms. Perfect for a hungry curlew!

I imagined how it would be if the curlews flew all the way from Siberia to find the mudflats gone. They would land on grass among holiday cabins, and they wouldn't have the energy to go anywhere else. They would starve!

At that moment, I heard the sound of car doors slamming. Mayor Potter strode towards us with Barry Bragg and his little dog following behind.

Barry Bragg was waving his arms and stamping his feet. "Flies!" he exclaimed. "And ants!"

Mayor Potter had brought a little camping stool and a pair of binoculars. Once she was settled, she held the binoculars up to her eyes and slowly scanned the mudflats.

I held my breath, waiting.

And waiting.

At last, Mayor Potter looked at me and said, "I can see a lot of seagulls, but I don't see any curlews, Claire!"

Archie was anxiously scanning the mudflats as well, but he didn't say anything. It was clear the birds had gone.

A sick feeling settled in the pit of my stomach. "But … but they were here," I stammered.

A look of doubt crossed Mayor Potter's face. "I'd like to believe you," she said. "But perhaps you've made a mistake."

Barry Bragg swished at a fly. "We've wasted enough time here," he said, turning to go. "The development will start in the morning. That's final!"

As the mayor's car drove away, my heart sank. I had promised to save the mudflats, but now all hope was lost.

Suddenly, Archie grabbed my arm. "Look up!" he gasped.

High overhead, dark shapes were circling. In the quiet, I could hear their mournful cries. Curlews!

"Something must have disturbed them," said Archie.

I had an image of Barry Bragg waving his arms and stamping his feet. He must have scared the curlews away.

And now it was too late to save them.

Chapter 5

The Protest

"I am not giving up," I said to Archie that night as we ate dinner. "Let's organise a protest at the mudflats."

Archie nodded. "It's our only chance," he said, through a mouthful of pasta. "But we need people to join us."

"I saw a notice posted on the community web page earlier today. There's a birdwatching group in the next town," Mum said. "They might join a protest."

Mum was right. The next morning, a crowd gathered in the car park near the mudflats. Some were there to watch the bulldozers in action, and some were protestors from the bird group.

Archie and I had made some signs that said, "SAVE THE CURLEWS".

Barry Bragg stood in front of a bulldozer while Snapper ran around chasing flies. A TV crew was setting up in front of Mr Bragg. He planned to make a speech before the machinery roared into action. Beside him stood Mayor Potter, smiling at the camera.

"Good morning, everyone," began Barry Bragg.

"Save the curlews!" yelled someone from the bird group.

Barry Bragg's voice trailed away as the camera swung towards our protest. We were on TV!

I took a deep breath and chanted:

"Two, four, six, eight,

The birds don't want your real estate!"

Suddenly, a microphone was thrust in front of me. "What's this protest about?" asked the woman from the TV station.

I felt my heart racing, but I knew what I had to do. In a shaky voice, I explained everything I knew about the curlews. "They need the mudflats so they can fatten up before they fly back to Siberia," I said. "Otherwise, they'll starve!"

Barry Bragg quickly stepped in front of the camera. “There is no proof these birds are here,” he said in a cross voice. “No proof at all!”

There was a moment of silence. Then, suddenly, I heard a dog barking excitedly as it raced across the mudflats.

Snapper had grown tired of chasing flies and had found something more exciting to chase.

You guessed it!

“Eastern curlews!” cried someone in the bird group.

At the same time, the TV camera zoomed in on the birds as they swooped over our heads.

Chapter 6

Cur-lew!

Did Archie and I save the mudflats? The short answer is: YES! The long answer is: YEEEEEEEEES!

After his TV appearance, Barry Bragg changed his mind about building a holiday park. He knew the community would no longer support it. Instead, his company built bird hides along the edge of the mudflats. These were little huts that people could sit in quietly to watch the birds.

Tourists came from everywhere to see the curlews, and they spent lots of money in Mud Crab Bay. Soon, Bay Side Constructions was busy building a brand-new hotel in town.

A year later, in early spring, Archie and I rode out to the mudflats to see if the curlews had arrived. As we settled into a bird hide, a shadow passed overhead. We watched in awe as a curlew swooped in low. Extending its long legs, it landed on the mud and snatched up a crab.

Cur-lew! it cried as it flew away. *Cur-lew!*

Archie and I smiled at one another. Everything was just as it should be.